A TOTALLY CLASSIC PICTURE BOOK
based on the film written and directed by Amy Heckerling

Adapted by G. M. BERROW
Illustrated by HEATHER BURNS

RP | KIDS
PHILADELPHIA

Running Press Kids
Hachette Book Group
1290 Avenue of the Americas, New York, NY 10104
www.runningpress.com/rpkids
@RP_Kids

Printed in China

First Edition: September 2020

Published by Running Press Kids, an imprint of Perseus Books, LLC, a subsidiary of Hachette Book Group, Inc. The Running Press Kids name and logo is a trademark of the Hachette Book Group.

The Hachette Speakers Bureau provides a wide range of authors for speaking events. To find out more, go to www.hachettespeakersbureau.com or call (866) 376-6591.

The publisher is not responsible for websites (or their content) that are not owned by the publisher.

Print book cover and interior design by Frances J. Soo Ping Chow
Cover and interior illustrations by Heather Burns

Library of Congress Control Number: 2019952131

ISBNs: 978-0-7624-7058-7 (hardcover), 978-0-7624-7059-4 (ebook), 978-0-7624-7117-1 (ebook), 978-0-7624-7074-7 (ebook)

APS

10 9 8 7 6 5 4 3 2 1

Cher Horowitz lived in a big, bright house in Beverly Hills,
but she actually had a way normal life for a kid.

Every morning, she would wake up, brush her teeth, and pick out her school clothes.

Daddy was very busy with work,
so Cher rode to school with her best friend, Dionne.

"Girlfriend!" Dionne squealed.
They had both chosen to wear plaid today.
They did their secret high-five, ending with a hair flip.

Once they arrived at Bronson Alcott Elementary,
Cher and Dionne strutted down the hall as if
it was their own personal runway.

"Where is your outfit from?" asked Amber.
Cher wasn't about to reveal her secrets.
As if!

"Excuse me, Miss Dionne!"
Their friend Murray giggled as he stepped aside for the fashionistas.

In class, Miss Geist had everyone take their seats for roll call.

"Cher?"
"Present!"

"Summer?"
"Here!"

CHER
SUMMER
CHRISTIAN
ELTON
TRAVIS
DIONNE

AM PM

"Christian?"
"Ring-a-ding, kid."

"Elton?"

But there was no answer. Elton had forgotten his cranberry juice
on the playground and had snuck outside to retrieve it.

And as usual, Travis Birkenstock was tardy,
but luckily he arrived just in time to see Miss Geist
introduce a brand new student.

"Everyone, this is Tai Fraser. She just moved here!"
Cher and Dionne thought Tai's baggy jeans were an interesting look
(and not in a good, faux-fur-backpack-and-purple-clogs kind of way).

At recess, Cher and Dionne noticed that Tai was sitting by herself.
She was watching the skateboarders, but they thought
she looked lonely and a bit clueless.

"That girl is begging for a makeover," said Cher.
"She could be a farmer in those clothes!" Dionne agreed.

Cher and Dionne loved doing stuff for other people.
Maybe Tai could be their new project!

At lunch, Cher and Dionne invited Tai to sit at their table.
"You guys are super-duper nice!" she chirped.
Cher beamed with pride.

After school, Cher and Dionne brought Tai to the mall.
With a little help, Tai was starting to look fashionable.

But the next day at lunch, Tai was nowhere to be found.
Cher and Dionne looked everywhere for her.

Finally, they found Tai with Amber.
"Tai and I are going to become the best painters in the school!"

Tai's Martian painting was cute, but Amber's painting was a bit
of a Monet (from far away, it was okay—but up close it was a big old mess).

After that, everyone had lots of ideas
for new things Tai could try.

"Photography!" said Elton.

"Dancing!" insisted Summer.

"Skateboarding?" suggested Travis.

"Whatever, Travis!" said Cher.
Thank goodness Tai had her new friends to save her.

Playing tennis was a much more appropriate way
to spend recess than riding a silly skateboard.

"Isn't this totally fun?" Dionne asked.

Suddenly, a tennis ball flew straight at Tai's nose!

"Ouch!" she cried out.
Everyone rushed over to make sure Tai was okay.

Tai was just fine but still seemed like she was buggin'.
"What's up, Tai?" Dionne asked.
"Come on, tell us," urged Cher.

Tai admitted that even though she had fun dressing up with Cher and Dionne . . .

painting with Amber . . .

photographing with Elton . . .

and dancing with Summer . . .
she could only think about one thing . . .

"...Skateboarding!"

Cher felt like the clueless one now.
Why hadn't she seen it before?

Tai was totally, majorly, crazy in love with skateboarding!
And that was cool. Tai should do whatever stuff she liked!

Cher was happy that Tai was happy.
But she and Dionne missed their shopping buddy.
"I hope Tai will still come to the mall
with us sporadically," said Cher.

Suddenly, Cher felt a tap on her shoulder. It was Tai!
"You think I would totally ditch my new friends? As if!"